This book is dedicated to our very own Dr. White!

Dear Dr. White,
You are such a blessing! Your encouragement, support, and knowledge has given me the confidence and strength needed to tackle any health issue that has come our way. Your ability to stay calm and listen to our concerns is irreplaceable. Thank you for accepting us with open arms. You have a special way of making my little ones feel like they are the most important patients of the day. I wanted to write this book for you to thank you for working so hard for all of your patients and especially for truly loving my kids.

With love,
Becky Carlyle

www.mascotbooks.com

Baby Silly Sickies

For more information, please contact:
Mascot Books
620 Herndon Parkway, Suite 320
Herndon, VA 20170
info@mascotbooks.com

Library of Congress Control Number: 2020901191

CPSIA Code: PRT2002A
ISBN-13: 978-1-64543-308-8

Printed in the United States

BABY SILLY SICKIES

Becky Carlyle

Illustrated by

Chiara Civati

I'm here at the doctor to find
out what's wrong with me.
I'm feeling kind of funny. What could it be?

Hello, Doctor White!
Will you see if I'm alright?
Many things seem wrong,
but I'm trying to stay strong.

I think I have puppy dogs in my ears,
and I started crying big green tears.

I might have purple polka dots on my skin,
and I'm definitely growing a little fish fin.

Yesterday, my heart was beeping,
and my legs were totally sleeping.

My hair is turning bright pink!
Not to mention, my hands *really* stink!

My tummy feels all lumpy,
and my elbows are bumpy.

My nose has been itchy.
My lips have been twitchy.

When you look in my throat,
do you see a sailboat?
When you look in my eye,
do you see a pumpkin pie?

Oh no—what did you find?
Is this all just in my mind?
Please try to be quick;
I'm afraid I'm really sick!

"Oh baby, your doctor says
you're doing just fine.
Did you know, she's very
glad you're mine?

Your doctor takes good care of you.
She loves you dearly, just like I do!"

Thank you, Doctor, for making sure I'm okay.
Let's go home, Mom. I'm ready to play!

"Alright you two, I hope your
day is happy and bright."

See you next time; we love you too, Doctor White!

ABOUT THE AUTHOR

Becky is a trained mezzo-soprano singer and holds a Bachelor of Music degree from Iowa State University. As a former K-12 vocal music teacher and youth symphony manager, Becky has spent her career enriching children educationally, creatively, and artistically. Becky has spent years writing grants, initially as part of her previous manager position, and continues to write on a case-by-case basis.

Now as a stay-at-home mom and freelance writer/photographer for a local newspaper, Becky still enjoys singing, but above all she is passionate about being a wife, mom, and friend. Experiencing life with children has given Becky a deeper perspective on what's most important in life. After publishing her first children's picture book, *Baby Squashy Face*, Becky realized she wasn't ready for the journey to end. She felt that a series could be developed from babies within the neighborhood. Becky hopes *Baby Silly Sickies* helps children feel more comfortable at the doctor and encourages children to speak up if anything is bothering them. She wants to let children know that their doctor cares about them!

ABOUT THE ILLUSTRATOR

Chiara Civati is a children's illustrator based out of Italy, where she lives and works in a small town on Como Lake. After studying fashion and textile design in high school, Chiara went on to study visual design and illustration at her college in Milan. Chiara eagerly started her work illustrating books and writing stories for children right after graduation, and hasn't stopped since.

She has been known to illustrate and publish her own stories that she's written, but more often, she spends her time working as a freelance illustrator which is what she loves most. When she's not busy at work, she loves to read books, especially fairy tales, and loves to travel around the world so she can continue being inspired by everything the world has to offer.